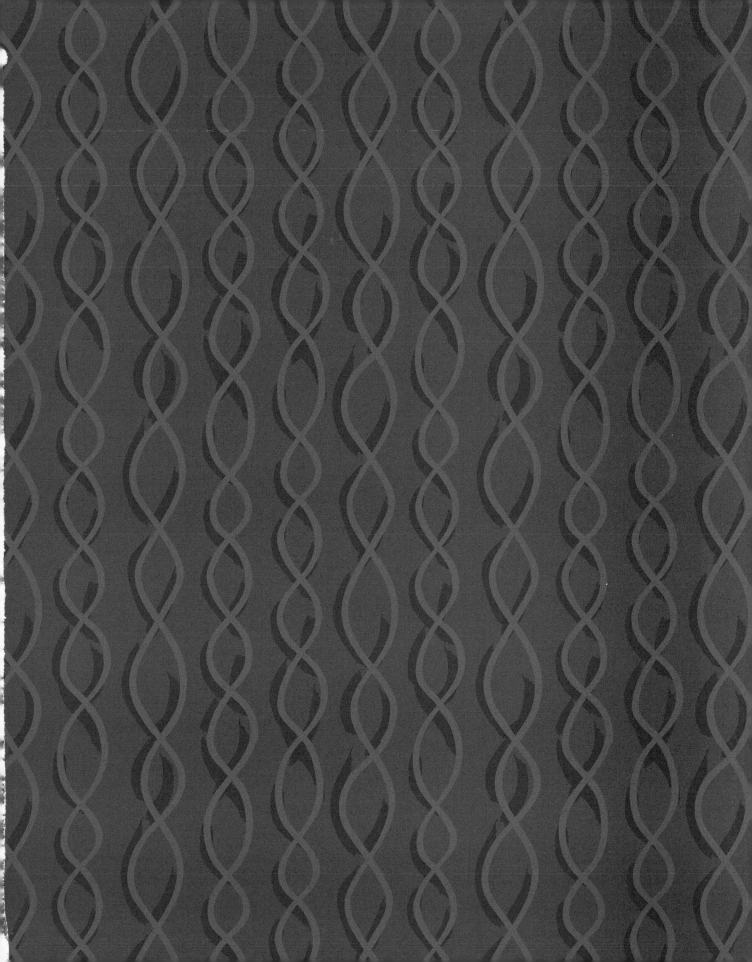

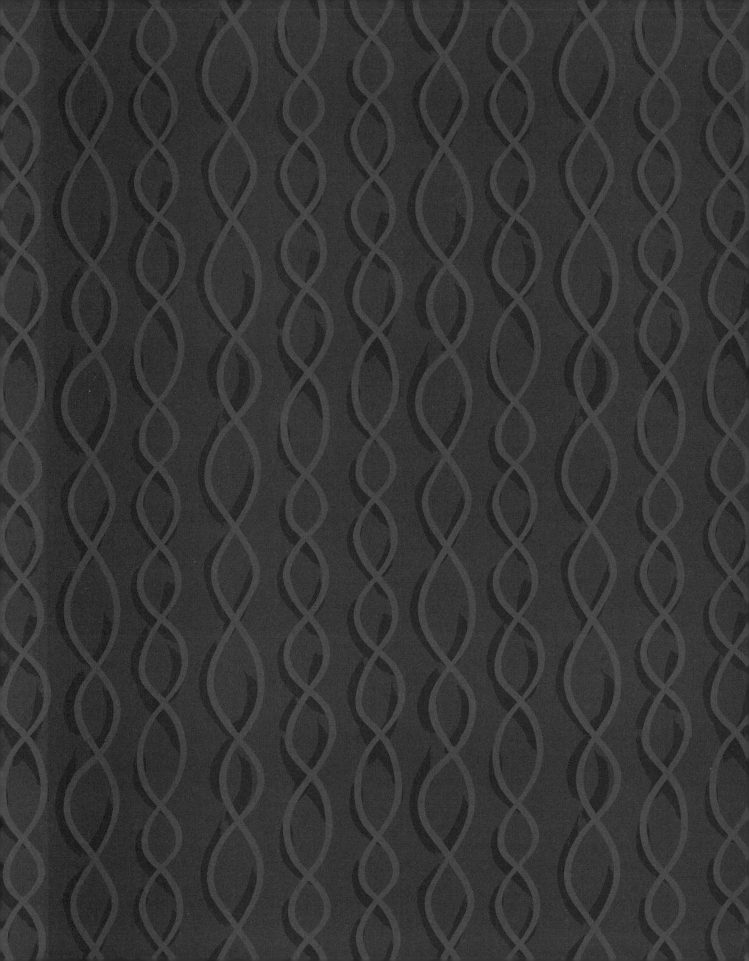

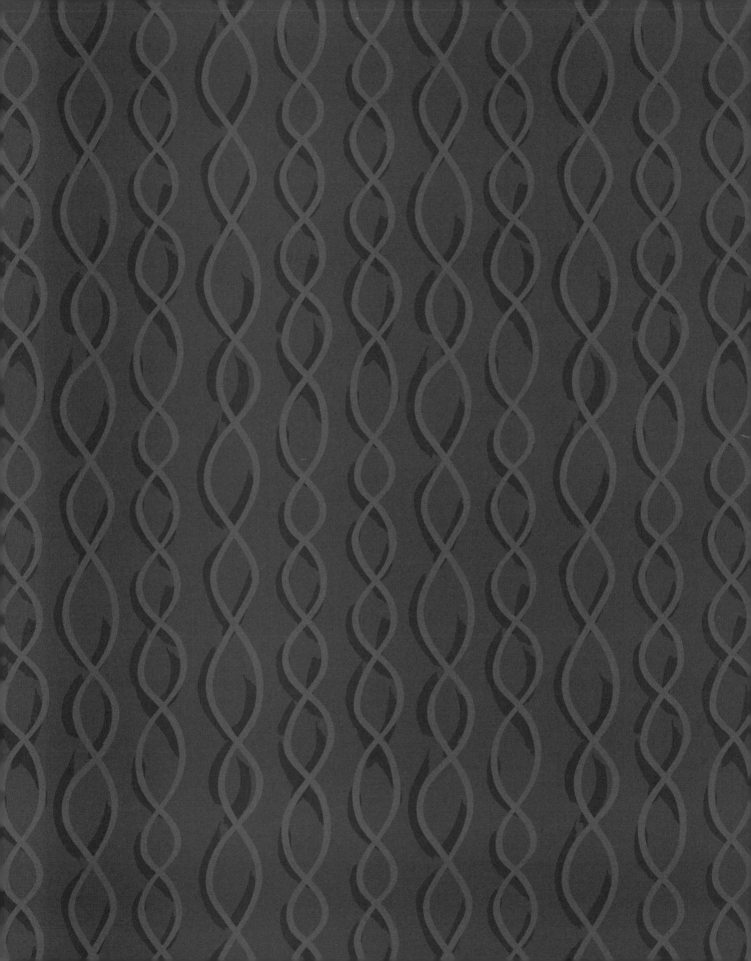

DISNEY

Countdown to Christmas

A Story a Day

DISNEY PRESS

Los Angeles • New York

Unless otherwise noted, all illustrations by the Disney Storybook Art Team. All rights reserved. Pixar properties © Disney/Pixar. Published by Disney Press, an imprint of Disney Book Group. No part of this book may be reproduced or transmitted in any form or by any means, electronic or mechanical, including photocopying, recording, or by any information storage and retrieval system, without written permission from the publisher.
For information address Disney Press, 1101 Flower Street, Glendale, California 91201.
Printed in the United States of America
First Hardcover Edition, September 2017
Library of Congress Control Number: 2015955214
10 9 8 7 6 5 4 3 2
ISBN: 978-1-4847-3052-2
FAC-038091-18071
For more Disney Press fun, visit www.disneybooks.com

Contents

Christmas in Never Land

Wendy sighed as she looked around the Lost Boys' hideout. "It's almost Christmas back home. I wish we weren't missing it."

"What's a Christmas?" Peter asked.

"Christmas is a time to show people how much you care for them," Wendy said. "And there's always a beautiful tree covered with lights."

"And lots of presents!" Michael chimed in.

"Don't forget the Christmas crackers," John added. "They make such a wonderful *kaboom* when they explode!"

Peter had an idea. He sent Wendy to collect seashells and then gathered the Lost Boys together. "We're going to surprise Wendy and have Christmas right here in Never Land!" he said.

"But how?" John asked.

Peter grinned. "Follow me!"

Peter and the Lost Boys went to see their friend Tiger Lily.

"We need presents for Christmas," Peter told the princess. "Do you have any ideas?"

"I know just the thing," Tiger Lily replied.

While Tiger Lily helped Peter make a beaded necklace for Wendy, her father taught the Lost Boys how to make arrowheads.

Peter and the Lost Boys wrapped the presents in large leaves. Then they went to the *Jolly Roger*.

"Peter, why are we here?" John asked.

"I'm going to swipe some powder from their cannons to make our Christmas crackers!" Peter explained.

Next Peter and the Lost Boys scouted the forest for the perfect Christmas tree and decorations. Soon the Lost Boys had transformed the hideout. Beneath the decorated tree stood piles of presents and stacks of homemade Christmas crackers. But something was still missing.

"The lights!" Peter exclaimed. "Where are the lights?"

"We may have to do without them," John said.

"There's got to be some way to light that tree," Peter said.

Tinker Bell put her hands on her hips and jingled at him.

"Not now, Tink. I'm trying to think," he said.

Peter came up with plan after plan, but none of them worked. He tried to borrow some glowing fish from Mermaid Lagoon, but the fish couldn't live out of the water. He tried to use fireflies to light the tree, but the pesky bugs just flew away.

"Now, now. It's still a very nice tree," John said. "Even if it is getting too dark to see it properly."

"It's no use," Peter said, defeated. "Without lights, what's the point in a tree? Christmas is ruined."

At that, Tinker Bell marched right up to him and started jingling as loudly as she could. Peter Pan's eyes grew wide. "*You* can make the tree light up?" he exclaimed. "Why didn't you say so before?"

Moments later, Wendy returned to an unusually dark hideout. "Hello?" she called. "Where is everyone?"

Suddenly, a glow filled the room and the Christmas tree began to sparkle with pixie dust. Wendy gasped as Peter Pan and the Lost Boys burst out of their hiding places. "Merry Christmas, Wendy!" they cheered.

Wendy beamed. Christmas had come to Never Land after all.

December 2

A Christmas to Remember

It was a cold December morning. Snow White was out feeding the birds and her other forest friends. Inside, Doc gathered the other Dwarfs. "Christmas is coming," he said. "What do you say we give Snow White a gifty nift—er—a nifty gift?"

The Dwarfs thought that was a fine idea! But what should they get her? Sleepy thought perhaps Snow White could use a new quilt for her bed. Sneezy suggested a lace handkerchief. Then Bashful spoke up.

"I have an idea," he said, blushing. "Why not give her something from our mines?"

"We could make her a crown," Happy said.

The next day, the Dwarfs busied themselves at the mine. Meanwhile, in their little cottage, Snow White got ready for Christmas, too. First she made a tray of special cookies shaped like bells and hearts and stars and Christmas trees. Then, while the cookies baked, she went into the forest and cut down a dwarf-sized pine tree.

When Snow White returned to the little cottage, it was filled with the smell of warm cinnamon and sugar. The smell was so delicious it made Snow White quite hungry. But instead of nibbling on the freshly baked cookies, she laced them on ribbons and hung them on the little pine tree. Then she draped strings of berries on the branches and decked the cottage with holly and mistletoe.

Snow White admired her handiwork. She hoped the Dwarfs liked the holiday treats and decorations.

When the Dwarfs came home and saw the tree, they danced and shouted with delight.

"Merry Christmas!" Snow White exclaimed. "I'm so happy you like my surprise!"

"We have a little surprise for you, too," Doc said. He took a small package wrapped in purple paper and tied with a big, golden bow out of his cloak and placed it under the tree. "No squeaking—er—peeking," he said.

On Christmas Eve, Snow White cooked a feast of roast fowl. All night, she kept looking at the package beneath the tree. Her stepmother, the evil Queen, had never given her anything. This was her very first Christmas present.

At last, the meal was finished, and the Dwarfs had washed all the dishes. Doc handed Snow White the small bundle.

When she opened it, Snow White gasped with delight. "Why, this is lovely!"

"We made it," said Happy proudly.

"We hope you—achoo!—like it!" said Sneezy.

Snow White went to the mirror and put on the crown. "Oh, thank you," she said. "This is wonderful—and it is even more precious because you put your hearts into it."

"Shucks, it wasn't much," said Bashful.

"But it is," Snow White cried. "You've made my first Christmas very memorable."

Snow White wore the splendid crown all through the Christmas holiday. Then she wrapped it carefully and tucked it away. She hoped she would have another occasion to wear it soon.

A Toy Christmas

"All right, everyone, settle down," Woody said. "Christmas is coming up and Andy and his family are going on vacation to the Grand Canyon. That means Christmas without Andy this year. It will just be us toys until January."

The toys fell silent. Christmas without Andy? What was the point of Christmas without a kid to share it with?

Buzz Lightyear walked over to where Woody was standing. "Come on, guys," he said. "Will it be the same without Andy? No. But we can still make it special. Cheer up! This year will be just for us. We'll have a toy Christmas!"

Woody looked at the other toys. "Buzz is right," he said. "We'll have a great Christmas this year."

Andy and his family left the next day, and the toys started getting ready for Christmas. They made decorations, practiced singing songs, and looked for presents for each other. Woody was glad his friends were in the holiday spirit, but he couldn't stop thinking about how much he missed Andy. How could they possibly have a fun Christmas without him?

"Hey, Woody, check out our Christmas tree!" Slinky Dog shouted. He pointed to a tree made entirely of cotton balls. It was hung with ribbons, and the Little Green Aliens were making garland out of buttons. There were even presents under the tree. It was very festive.

Woody smiled a little bit. He was impressed at how hard the toys were working to

make Christmas a happy holiday. Everyone had really gotten into the spirit!

Finally, it was the big day. The toys all gathered together to celebrate, but Woody was still thinking of Andy.

"Hey, Sheriff, why so down? It's Christmas Eve!" Buzz said. "It's time to celebrate."

"It's just not the same without Andy," Woody said.

"You're right," Buzz said. "But you have other friends besides Andy. Come on."

Buzz led Woody over to the Christmas tree. Suddenly, there was a jolly "Ho, ho, rrrrroar!" as RC Car rolled into the room. RC was decorated to look like a sleigh. He even had a jingle bell tied to his antenna. Right behind him was Rex, with a white cotton beard and a red sock hat.

"Sorry about the roar," Rex said. "Sometimes I forget I'm Santa Claus, not a fierce bone-crunching carnivorous dinosaur!"

Rex went to the tree. One by one he handed presents to each and every toy.

Woody looked at his friends. Buzz was right. Christmas without Andy wasn't better or worse. It was just different. Spending time with people—and toys—you loved was what Christmas was really all about. And he had the best friends any toy could ask for.

"Hey, everyone, look!" Slinky Dog yelled, pointing to the window. Outside, snow drifted down. "It's a white Christmas!" he shouted.

Woody smiled. "Merry Christmas, everyone!"

A Present for the Queen

Alice was watching some children build a snowman outside. It was rather warm in her house, and soon, she grew quite sleepy. Suddenly, something hopped across the snow in front of her house. "Why, it's the White Rabbit!" she cried.

Alice ran after the rabbit. "You're always running," she said when she caught up with him. "Whatever is wrong this time?"

"I've lost the Queen's Christmas present," the White Rabbit cried. "If I don't find it, she'll have my head!" Then, without another word, he dove down a hole.

Alice hurried after him and found herself on a snowy path lined with evergreen trees. The White Rabbit was gone, but Alice could see his footprints in the snow. She decided to follow them.

All at once, the footprints stopped. "I've lost him again," Alice said with a sigh.

"Lost who?" someone asked.

A toothy smile appeared in one of the trees, followed quickly by a purple striped cat that materialized around the smile.

"Cheshire Cat!" Alice cried happily. "The White Rabbit has lost the Queen's present, and—"

"But that's a lost *what*," the cat interrupted. "I thought you said you lost a *who*."

"I didn't lose a what," she said. "The White Rabbit did. And now *I've* lost *him*."

"Well, I can't help you with your who, but I *can* help you with your lost what. Try the Mad Hatter."

Alice followed the path until she found the Mad Hatter. "Ah, Alice," he said. "We were just singing Christmas Harolds."

"Don't you mean Christmas carols?" Alice asked.

"What does Carol have to do with it?" asked the March Hare. "Everyone knows Harold wrote the best Christmas songs!"

Alice shook her head. She had no time for the hatter's nonsense. "I need your help," she told him. "The Queen's present is lost!"

With a twinkle in his eye, the Mad Hatter took off his hat. Sitting atop his head was a large box wrapped in Christmas paper. And on *top* of that was the Dormouse! Scooping up the Dormouse, the hatter handed the present to Alice.

Alice thanked him and went on her way. Soon the White Rabbit's footprints reappeared! Alice followed them all the way to the Queen's castle, where the White Rabbit was apologizing to the Queen.

"I-I'm sorry, I lost your present—" he said.

"I found it!" Alice interrupted.

The Queen glared at Alice. "Off with her head!" she yelled.

"Perhaps you should open the gift first, dear," the King suggested meekly.

"I suppose I could," the Queen said, tearing off the box's wrapping. Her eyes lit up as she pulled a small Christmas tree out of the box.

As the Queen of Hearts admired her present, a large grin appeared in the air next to Alice.

"Now might not be the worst time to slip away," said the Cheshire Cat.

Alice snuck out of the room and began to run. But she slipped on a patch of ice and hit her head.

When Alice opened her eyes, she found herself back at home. She yawned sleepily. "What a strange dream I've just had," she said.

Stretching, Alice looked out the window. The snowman was finished, and it was holding a teacup. Alice frowned. Perhaps it hadn't been a dream after all. . . .

December 5

Donald's Christmas Tree

It was the day before Christmas. Donald had baked cookies. He had wrapped gifts. Now all he needed was a Christmas tree.

Donald put on his coat and cap. He grabbed his ax. "Come on, Pluto," he said. "We're going to find our tree."

Pluto and Donald went deep into the woods. Donald looked left. He looked right. Then he saw it: the perfect tree! Donald picked up his ax and went to work.

"TIMBER!" Donald cried as the tree toppled over and landed in the snow.

Inside the tree, two chipmunks named Chip and Dale held on for dear life. They lived in the tree Donald had chosen!

"Come on, Pluto," called Donald. "Let's take our tree home."

Home through the woods went Donald Duck, dragging the tree behind him. At home, he set up the tree. He hung ornaments on the branches and strung tinsel all over the tree.

"There!" Donald said when the job was done. "Doesn't that look fine? Now I just need the gifts. You stay here, Pluto. I'll be right back."

As soon as Donald was out of sight, Chip and Dale left their hiding place. They danced on the branches until the needles quivered. They made faces at themselves in the shiny colored balls, tugged on the tinsel and twisted the lights, and laughed until their little sides shook.

"Grrr," growled Pluto disapprovingly. But Chip and Dale did not care. Chip just picked off a shiny ball and threw it at Pluto!

Pluto jumped and barely caught it in his teeth.

At that moment, Donald came back into the room. "Pluto!" he cried. "Bad dog!" He thought Pluto had been snatching balls from the tree.

"Now be good," said Donald, "while I bring in the rest of the presents."

No sooner was Donald out of sight than Chip and Dale appeared again. *Plunk!* Chip's head went through a colored ball. Dale laughed and laughed at the funny sight. But Pluto did not think it was funny at all. They were going to spoil Donald's tree!

Pluto growled, but the naughty chipmunks did not stop. He knew he had to do something. Pluto got set to jump.

"Pluto!" cried Donald from the doorway. "What is the matter with you? If you can't behave, you'll have to go out to your doghouse for the rest of Christmas Eve."

Just then, up in the treetop, Chip grew tired of wearing his round golden mask. He pulled off the ball and let it drop.

Crash!

"What was that?" cried Donald, looking at the tree.

Dale began to play with the colored lights, twisting them so they turned off and on.

Donald peered among the branches until he spied Chip and Dale.

"Well, well," he chuckled, lifting them down. "So you're the mischief-makers. And to think I blamed poor Pluto. I'm sorry, Pluto."

Pluto marched to the front door and held it open. He felt Chip and Dale should go out in the snow.

"Oh, Pluto!" cried Donald. "It's Christmas Eve. We must be kind to everyone. The spirit of Christmas is love, you know."

So Pluto made friends with Chip and Dale. And when Mickey and Minnie came to the house for caroling, they all agreed that this was by far the happiest Christmas Eve they had ever had.

December 6

Cookies for Santa

"It's going to be Christmas soon," little Tiana said. She was watching her daddy make dinner. Nobody cooked like Tiana's daddy. One day he hoped to open his own restaurant. And he was teaching Tiana everything he knew!

"Already?" Daddy said with a sly grin. "Wasn't it just Christmas last year?"

Tiana laughed. "Don't be silly, Daddy," she said. "This is important!"

"We'd better listen, then," Tiana's mama said.

Tiana's daddy put down his spoon and turned to his daughter. "Okay," he said. "I'm listening."

"Santa's going to visit," Tiana explained. "On Christmas Eve. I want to make him some cookies, but I can't decide what kind to make."

"Aren't you a little small to be making cookies?" Mama asked.

"No!" Tiana and her daddy both said at once.

Mama laughed. "My mistake," she said.

"See, there's chocolate chip cookies," Tiana said. "And ginger snaps. And oatmeal. And snickerdoodles. . . ."

"Mmm," Mama said.

"And peppermint bark and peanut butter cookies," Tiana went on. "And shortbread, and . . ."

"You know your way around the kitchen already, baby," Tiana's daddy told her. "You could make any of those."

"I know," Tiana said. "But none of them seem right."

"You know," Mama said, "I think Santa deserves a real New Orleans—style welcome. You should make him something he can't get anywhere else."

Tiana's eyes widened. "Beignets!" she said. "That's it! Thanks, Mama!"

On Christmas Eve, Tiana got out a big bowl and her daddy's big wire whisk. She measured out the ingredients and got the dough mixed up all by herself, even though she had to stand on a stepstool to reach the table. Then her daddy helped her fry the pillowy little beignets. Finally, Tiana tossed them in powdered sugar.

"Whew! That was a lot of work," Tiana told her daddy. "Your whisk is really heavy! I hope Santa likes the beignets!"

"They look perfect," Tiana's father told her, kissing the top of her head. He popped one of the beignets into his mouth. "Mmm, and they taste perfect, too," he said.

"Hey!" Tiana said, batting his hands away from the plate. "Those are for Santa!"

"And he's going to love them," Tiana's daddy said proudly.

That night, Tiana went to bed, happy with the gift she'd left for Santa. When she woke up in the morning, she ran to the kitchen. The plate was empty! Just a dusting of powdered sugar remained. Next to the plate was a single brightly wrapped present. The label said: TO TIANA, FROM SANTA. THANK YOU FOR THE SNACK. IT WAS DELICIOUS!

Inside was a brand-new whisk, bright and shining and perfectly sized for little Tiana to bake anything she wanted!

"It's wonderful!" she cried happily. "I'm going to make beignets all the time now!"

Tiana's daddy smiled. "Seems to me this was the perfect gift for all of us, then."

A Gift for WALL·E

WALL·E and EVE peeked over the top of a pile of garbage. The humans had been back on Earth for several months. Now they were doing something the robots had never seen them do before. In fact, the robots thought the humans were acting very strange. Two men were stringing colored lights along a fence, and a woman was decorating a tree with glass balls. Another man was setting up a plastic statue of a fat white-bearded man in a red suit.

WALL·E looked closely at the humans. Whatever they were doing seemed to be making them very happy. And if it made the humans happy, maybe it would make the robots happy, too. That gave WALL·E an idea.

WALL·E and his friends went to work looking for ways to copy the humans. Some of the bots picked up tinsel and colored paper left by the humans. Others collected strings of colored lights and crates of packing peanuts.

EVE was looking for decorations when she heard one of the humans say, "I just love Christmas." *Christmas!* Was this the name for what the humans were doing?

"Yes," said the Captain. "But don't forget, Christmas isn't about things. It's about showing your friends and family that you care."

The words hummed inside EVE. Robots didn't have family, but they *did* have friends. And she had one friend who meant more to her than any other—WALL·E. She needed to show him that she appreciated him.

But what kind of present would do that?

EVE roamed far and wide. Then, far from WALL E's trailer, her gaze locked on the perfect present.

On Christmas Eve, the bots held a big celebration, just like the humans. The umbrella-bot wore a pointy red hat with a pom-pom on top. The robots beeped out words to the songs they had heard the humans singing.

While the other bots celebrated, EVE pulled WALL·E aside. She held out a present wrapped in pretty patterned paper.

WALL·E looked surprised. "Ee-vah?" he asked. EVE nodded.

WALL·E admired how the shiny paper shimmered in the colored lights. He had never seen anything so pretty.

Open it, EVE signaled. WALL·E carefully unwrapped the present. He folded up each scrap of paper and laid it on the ground next to him. Finally, he pulled away the last piece.

In his hand, WALL·E held a little evergreen, a miniature Christmas tree. The longer version of EVE's name was Extra-terrestrial Vegetation Evaluator. She had been trained to find plants and was drawn to the little tree. She knew that WALL·E, with his kind ways and big heart, would take care of this present better than anyone.

Together, WALL·E and EVE dug a hole in the earth and planted the little Christmas tree.

WALL·E placed a shiny silver star on top. The star twinkled brightly.

EVE reached out her hand. WALL·E took it. "Ee-vah," he said.

Now he understood why humans liked Christmas so much.

The Wonderful Winter Tree

One cold winter morning, Bambi awoke to find the world covered in a soft white blanket. "What is it, Mother?" he asked, gazing around in wonder.

"This is snow," replied Bambi's mother. "It's finally winter."

Bambi took a cautious step, feeling the ice crunch under his hooves. "I like snow!" he said. "It's so . . . cold!"

Just then, Thumper hopped over. "Hiya, Bambi!" he called. "Wanna go sliding?"

Thumper led Bambi to the pond. It was completely frozen. The bunny slapped the ice with his foot. "It's all right," he told Bambi. "See? The water's stiff!"

Bambi saw his friend Flower the skunk. "Do you want to come sliding?" he asked.

Flower shook his head. "No thanks. I'm off to my den. I'm going to sleep through the winter." He yawned. "Good-bye, Bambi. See you in the spring!"

Bambi looked back at the pond. Thumper was sliding across the ice with ease. Bambi stepped on the ice. His hooves went sliding in four different directions!

"Kind of wobbly, aren't ya," Thumper said, laughing.

Sliding with Thumper made Bambi hungry, so he left to find his mother. In the past they had always been able to find food, but Bambi could see that it wasn't so easy in winter. Everything was covered with snow and ice. There was no green!

Eventually, Bambi's mother uncovered a small patch of grass for Bambi to eat. "Don't worry," she told him. "Winter doesn't last forever. Spring will come again soon enough."

By the end of December, it seemed like there was nothing left in the forest for Bambi to eat. The days grew short and the nights grew long, and throughout them Bambi's stomach rumbled. No matter how hard they searched, there was never enough food. Then one day, something truly amazing happened.

Thumper was the first to see it. "Hey, Bambi! Would you look at that tree?" he hollered.

There before them was a pine tree unlike any Bambi had ever seen. It was draped with strings of bright berries and yummy popcorn, and covered in ripe, juicy apples.

"Mother, look!" Bambi shouted.

Bambi's mother smiled down at her son. "What a special gift to have on your first Christmas," she said.

Thumper sniffed one of the apples.

Bambi pranced over and took a bite. The apple was delicious!

"Can we share this food with our friends, Mother?" he asked.

"Of course," she said. "Christmas is a time to share what we have with those we love."

As Bambi and Thumper danced happily around the tree, a gentle hush fell over the clearing. What a magical gift, thought Bambi. There was enough food on the tree to feed all the animals who were hungry. Winter was long and hard . . . but it turned out it was wonderful after all.

An Aristocat-ic Christmas

A heavy snowfall blanketed Paris. Duchess sat on the windowsill, gazing at the magical scene.

"Look, O'Malley. We're going to have a white Christmas!" she cried.

O'Malley sat up on his velvet chair. "Sure is pretty, Princess. But winter can be cold, and food is scarce."

The very thought of going hungry brought down O'Malley's spirits. He was happy living in Madame's mansion with his beloved Duchess and her three kittens: Berlioz, Toulouse, and Marie. But sometimes O'Malley felt guilty that he was warm and well-fed while his alley cat friends scavenged in trash cans. It just didn't seem fair.

"Wait till you see what Madame has prepared for the holiday," Duchess said. "It's always quite the celebration!"

But O'Malley wasn't listening. He was worried about his old friends. He wanted to see them again and make sure they were okay.

By Christmas Eve, the whole house glittered with Christmas cheer. "Isn't Christmas magnificent?" Duchess asked O'Malley. "Come, I'll show you the best part."

As they entered the kitchen, a host of heavenly smells prickled O'Malley's nose. Spicy puddings, apple tarts, roast goose.

"This *could* be the best part," O'Malley said.

"What do you mean, could be?" Duchess asked.

O'Malley smiled mischievously. He had a plan.

The next day brought a flurry of guests bearing

gifts for Madame. But she wasn't the only one to get gifts. Madame brought out three brightly colored bundles. The kittens eagerly tore into their presents. Toulouse got a new set of paints, Berlioz was given some new sheet music, and Marie received a silver bell necklace.

Soon it was time for Christmas dinner. But when everyone sat down at the dining table, O'Malley's seat was empty.

"Where can O'Malley be?" Duchess asked, worried.

Just then, she heard a great clatter at the front door. In strutted O'Malley, followed by his old friend Scat Cat and his band.

"Welcome!" Madame called. "And Merry Christmas to you all! Please, won't you join us? There is more than enough to go around."

As the band members happily sat down at the table, Madame rang for the butler. "You may now bring in the roast goose," she said with a smile. "But first, my guests must play for their supper."

Madame knew Scat Cat and his friends never turned down a chance to play! They happily started with "Jingle Bells" before moving on to "Deck the Halls." It was the jivey-est jingling that had ever jangled a Christmas Day.

Madame's guests were delighted. They were tired of stuffy dinner parties. This was the liveliest—and most unique— party they had been to in ages.

"Now, *this* is Christmas!" O'Malley declared.

And from the look of things, nobody disagreed.

Flik's Christmas Invention

Christmas was only a few days away. On top of its normal work, the ant colony was preparing for the Christmas celebration.

"We'll never get it all done!" Princess Dot said. "And even if we do, everyone is so tired, no one will be in the mood to celebrate."

"There must be a way to make it easier," Flik said thoughtfully. "Where does the most extra work come from at Christmastime?"

"Well, we *do* spend a lot of time wrapping and decorating presents," Dot replied.

Flik nodded. "I'll think of something!" he promised.

As the ant colony's official inventor, Flik worked hard to come up with new ways to make the ants' work easier. Dot knew if anyone could find a way to help the ants get through the Christmas rush, it was him!

On Christmas Eve, Flik showed Princess Dot and Queen Atta the gift-wrapping machine he invented. "This will save us time and make our work easier!" he said proudly.

Dot smiled. But Queen Atta wasn't impressed. "That's what Christmas is all about," she said. "Making an extra effort to please the people we love. Think of all you could have finished in the time it took you to make the machine."

Before Flik could respond, Atta left the room.

"Don't worry, Flik," Dot told him. "Wait until she sees this thing in action. Come on, let's start wrapping gifts."

Word about the wrapping machine spread quickly. The ants were thrilled. Atta may not have been impressed, but the other ants were eager for the help. They lined up to use the new invention on their presents. Flik carefully placed their gifts on the machine. His heart raced as he pulled the start lever and cranked the machine. In just a few minutes, everyone in the colony would be ready for Christmas!

Suddenly, Flik heard a strange noise. *Riiiip!* The conveyor belt jammed, the twigs snapped, and the machine crashed to the ground.

"Our gifts!" one of the ants cried.

The ants grumbled as they walked away from the mess Flik's invention had caused. Now that their presents had been ruined, they had even more work than before.

Flik hung his head. "Maybe Atta was right," he said.

"You were only trying to help," Dot said. "It's not too late, Flik. I have an idea about how you can make it up to everyone."

The next morning, Queen Atta and the ants found a curtain drawn across the colony's great hall. Flik was standing beside it, waiting for them.

"Merry Christmas!" he said, pulling back the curtain. "Come on in."

Behind the curtain was the most amazing feast anyone had ever seen.

Flik beamed. He had stayed up all night preparing his surprise—a Christmas feast with all the trimmings. He wanted to make up for the mess his invention had created.

"It was a lot of work," Flik said. "But work is fun when you're doing it with friends."

Flik smiled at Dot. At last he understood the true meaning of Christmas. Atta had been right after all.

Ghosts of Christmas Past

It should have been a joyous time. It was Rapunzel's first Christmas since coming home to Corona. But Rapunzel was not ready for a happy holiday. "No way," she said. "I refuse to celebrate Christmas! I had enough of it in the tower and now I'd like to forget it even exists!"

"What? Why?" cried Eugene.

Rapunzel shuddered at her memories of Christmases with Mother Gothel. "It's terrifying!" she explained. "All of those scary songs, the eerie stories of Nicholas the ghostly Christmas elf . . ."

Eugene looked at Rapunzel in disbelief. It was clear Mother Gothel had made Christmas sound frightening to make Rapunzel afraid of the world. Eugene couldn't wait to show her what Christmas was *really* about!

"Come on!" he said as he took Rapunzel outside. "Now, does this seem like a spooky holiday to you?"

In the courtyard, there were children singing Christmas carols and townsfolk decorating an enormous Christmas tree. Rapunzel looked at the tree, confused. "You'll need a lot more charms if you want to scare off the ghostly Christmas elf."

Eugene laughed. "These are ornaments," he said. "They're meant to make the tree look pretty."

Later Eugene read Rapunzel a book about St. Nicholas. "See, he isn't ghostly." Eugene showed

Rapunzel drawings of a smiling bearded man. He actually looked quite jolly.

Rapunzel's face lit up. To think all those Christmases she'd been afraid! Now she knew what she had been missing! "We have so much work to do!"

For weeks, Rapunzel lived and breathed Christmas. In the castle kitchen, she helped bake dozens and dozens of Christmas cookies. She learned every word of every Christmas carol she had never heard before. She decked every undecked inch of the halls with garlands and ribbon, and for the first time, she made beautiful—not spooky—Christmas ornaments. By the time Christmas Eve arrived, Rapunzel was exhausted but happy.

Rapunzel's father, the King, proposed a toast. "For years, our hearts have not felt whole." He smiled at Rapunzel.

The Queen raised her glass and added, "But now, for the first time, this holiday is a joyful one—for all of us."

Surrounded by her warm and loving family, Rapunzel could not imagine a better Christmas. "Thank you. For all of this," she told Eugene.

He smiled. After all those spooky, sleepless Christmas Eves in the tower, Rapunzel had certainly earned a peaceful holiday. And there would be many more like it.

12

Merry Christmas, Winnie the Pooh

One snowy Christmas Eve, Winnie the Pooh looked up and down, in and out, and all around his house. "I have a tree, some candles, and lots of decorations," he said, "but *something* seems to be missing."

Suddenly, a soft knocking sounded on Pooh's door. Perhaps whatever Pooh was missing was just outside!

Pooh opened the door. A small snowman stood shaking on his step.

"H-hello, P-Pooh," said the snowman in a shivery, quivery, but oh-so-familiar voice. "I do like Christmas, but I wish my ears wouldn't get so very cold."

Pooh invited the snowman in. After much melting by Pooh's cozy fireplace, the snowman looked less like a snowman and more like Piglet!

"My!" said Pooh, happy to see a friend where there used to be a snowman.

"My!" said Piglet, now warm enough to see Pooh's glowing Christmas tree. "Are you going to string popcorn for your tree?" he asked.

"I *had* popcorn and string," admitted Pooh. "But now there's only string."

"That's okay," Piglet said with a laugh. "We can use the string to wrap the presents you're giving."

At that, something began to tickle the brain of the little bear. "I forgot to get presents!" exclaimed Pooh.

"Don't worry, Pooh," said Piglet, trying to smile bravely. "It's the thought that counts."

Soon Piglet left to finish his own Christmas preparations. Pooh didn't know what to do about the forgotten presents, but he did know where to find help.

"Hello!" called Pooh, knocking on Christopher Robin's door.

"Come in, Pooh," said Christopher Robin, smiling.

Pooh stepped through the door and looked around. "What are those?" he asked, pointing to some stockings hung by the fireplace.

"Those are stockings to hold Christmas presents," explained Christopher Robin.

That reminded Pooh that he didn't have presents—*or* stockings.

Christopher Robin couldn't help with the gifts, but he happily gave Pooh stockings for himself and all his friends.

Pooh thanked Christopher Robin and hurried off to deliver the stockings. "I will get presents later," Pooh told himself. "The stockings come first." With a small note that said *From Pooh*, he left stockings for Piglet, Tigger, Rabbit, Eeyore, Gopher, and Owl.

Back at his own comfy house, Pooh said, "Now I must think about presents for my friends." But sleepy Pooh's thinking soon turned into dreaming.

The next morning, Pooh was awakened by a big and bouncy knock at his door. Pooh opened the door. It was his friends. They began to *thank* him!

"No more cold ears with my new stocking cap," said Piglet.

"My stripedy sleeping bag is Tigger-rific!" exclaimed Tigger.

"So is my new carrot cover," Rabbit chimed in.

Eeyore was particularly pleased with his new tail warmer.

"Something awfully nice is going on," said Pooh. "But I'm not sure how it happened."

"It's called Christmas, buddy bear," replied Tigger.

Then everyone gave their presents to Pooh: lots of pots of honey.

Surrounded by his friends and his favorite tasty treats, Pooh had to agree. "Christmas! What a sweet thought, indeed."

13

Aurora's Homemade Holiday

One snowy December day, Princess Aurora and Prince Phillip decided to go for a walk. "My aunts and I used to love getting ready for Christmas," Aurora told Phillip.

The fairies Flora, Fauna, and Merryweather had secretly raised Aurora to keep her safe from an evil fairy. Even though she now knew who she was, Aurora still thought of them as her aunts. "Let's invite them for the holidays," Phillip suggested.

"What a splendid idea!" Aurora cried.

That afternoon, Prince Phillip sent an invitation to Flora, Fauna, and Merryweather. Then he set off on a short trip to attend to some royal duties. Aurora didn't mind. Now her Christmas preparations would be a surprise for Phillip when he returned!

When the three good fairies arrived, the princess made her special request.

"You want a Christmas *exactly* like the ones we shared at the cottage?" Flora asked. "That means we can't use magic."

"You'd better take our wands so we're not tempted to use them," Fauna said to Aurora.

Aurora led the fairies to baskets of evergreen branches, ornaments, and bows.

"Let's start by trimming the tree!" exclaimed Merryweather.

"We should hang the evergreen branches first," Flora said.

Waiting for her two aunts to agree could take all day, so Aurora suggested that she and Flora put up the branches while Fauna and Merryweather decorated the tree.

Laterw Aurora and the fairies baked their special Christmas dessert. "I can't wait until Phillip tastes your lemon cake," Aurora told Fauna.

"I want to give Phillip a homemade present," Aurora said when they were done baking. "But I don't know how to sew. Can you help me?"

Aurora and the fairies spent the day making Phillip a new shirt. As Aurora worked on her present, she began to smile. "Do you remember the stockings you made when I was a little girl?" she asked with a giggle.

"Of course!" said Flora. "We forgot to stitch up the bottoms and the gifts fell out."

Aurora and the fairies laughed at the happy memory.

When Prince Phillip arrived back at the castle, Aurora met him at the door. "Close your eyes," she said, "and don't open them until I tell you to."

Aurora led Phillip into the grand hall, where the fairies were waiting. "Ready!" Aurora announced.

Phillip looked around. Crooked wreaths dangled from the walls. The Christmas tree was decorated only on one side. Lopsided cakes, burnt tarts, and misshapen cookies filled a table.

"I've never seen preparations like these before," Phillip said politely. "I can understand why you find them so . . . special."

Aurora handed Phillip his gift.

"A shirt!" said the prince, opening the box. As he put on his present, the princess and the fairies burst into laughter.

"Oh, dear. That's certainly not the right size," Aurora said.

"Nonsense!" Phillip insisted. "It's a perfect fit."

"Just like you and me," Aurora said to her prince. "Merry Christmas!"

December **14**

Present Problems!

It was the week before Christmas. Belle had almost finished gathering presents for her new friends in the Beast's castle, but she had a problem. She couldn't decide what to get the Beast. She wanted to give him the perfect gift, but what?

Belle went to the kitchen for Mrs. Potts's advice. She told Mrs. Potts about her problem, but the teapot was busy preparing for the large Christmas feast. "I think he needs a new brush!" Mrs. Potts suggested and then rushed off.

Belle wasn't so sure. A brush might be practical, but it wasn't very special. Maybe Cogsworth would have a better idea.

Belle raced up to the great hall, where Cogsworth was busy hanging holiday decorations. He wasn't much help, either.

"I think that repairs to the stable are in order," Cogsworth suggested. "He's neglected them for far too long. I'll organize it right away."

You're right, Cogsworth," Belle said. "The stables could use some work. But it's far too cold to do that in winter. And I'm not sure that would exactly be a gift to the Beast. But it sounds like a great idea for the spring!"

"Yes, yes, of course. More time for planning!" Cogsworth said, and he hustled away to start making plans.

Finally, Belle went to ask Lumiere's advice. The candelabrum was busy practicing a new song for Christmas Day.

"Lumiere, I need a present for the Beast. Do you have any ideas?" Belle asked.

"I think you should paint him a grand portrait! We need more portraits in the castle," Lumiere said. But Belle wasn't very good at painting, and she didn't think the Beast would sit still long enough for her to paint a picture of him.

Belle was discouraged. She went to the library to think. The Beast had given her the room as a gift. She loved exploring it, looking for new stories to read.

Belle climbed a ladder to a shelf at the very, very top of the library. She had never been up there before, and the books were covered with dust and cobwebs. Belle wiped away the grime from the spines of the books and began to smile. She knew just what to give the Beast!

On Christmas morning, Belle handed the Beast a small present. "Merry Christmas!" she said. "I hope you like it!"

The Beast gently opened the gift to reveal—a book!

"It's my favorite book," Belle told him. "I found it hidden away and forgotten in the library. I thought you might enjoy it."

The Beast smiled and held the book close. Then he handed it back to Belle. "Will you read it to me?" he asked.

Belle smiled, and the two settled down in front of a cozy fire in the library, where they spent the rest of the day reading the new book.

"The end," Belle said, finishing the story.

The Beast smiled. "Belle, this was the best Christmas present I ever received. Will you read it again?"

The Best Present Ever

"*Woooo-eeeee!*" Mater slid past his best buddy, Lightning McQueen. Christmas was just a few days away, and the two friends were sledding on Mater's junkyard sled. "This here's the best sled in Radiator Springs!" Mater exclaimed.

"I know, you've told me," Lightning said with a laugh.

"I can't wait to take it to Kersploosh Mountain!" Mater said. Kersploosh Mountain was a nearby water park. At this time of year, all the waterslides were frozen over.

"Uh, Mater, there's something I need to tell you," Lightning said. The race car looked worried. "They moved up that race I'm competing in. I won't be here for Christmas after all." Lightning shook his head. "I'm really sorry, buddy."

Later that afternoon, Mater saw a truck speeding around town with new tires. That gave him an idea. Maybe if he got Lightning a great Christmas present, they could celebrate the holidays early.

Mater raced after the truck. "What if I told you I had something that goes even faster than those tires?" he asked.

Curious, the truck agreed to hear him out.

Mater raced to his junkyard to grab his sled. "Here she is: superfast gliders and built-in bumper tires!" he said.

The truck was amazed. He happily traded the tires for Mater's sled.

The next day, Lightning and Mater exchanged gifts.

"Open yours, open yours, open yours!" Mater cried.

"Okay," Lightning said. "But Mater, I have some good news that . . ." Lightning trailed off as he unwrapped the tires. "You got these for me?" he asked.

Mater beamed. "If my best buddy can't be here for Christmas, then he'd sure as heck better win his race!"

"I love them," Lightning began, "but . . ."

Mater was already ripping open his gift. When he saw two tickets to Kersploosh Mountain, his eyes grew wide.

Lightning shrugged. "You're my best friend. And a trophy is just another trophy. I withdrew from the race. I'm staying here for Christmas!"

"This is awesome!" Mater exclaimed. "We're going to Kersploosh Mountain! We can take my sled and . . . uh-oh."

Lightning looked around. "Mater, where is your sled?" he asked.

Mater shuffled nervously. "Uh, I may have traded it to get you them there snow tires. I thought you could use them."

The two friends started laughing. "We thought we were getting each other the perfect Christmas presents, but we ended up getting stuff we can't use!" Lightning exclaimed.

"Yeah, but I'll tell you one thing, buddy," Mater said. "Spending Christmas together is still the best present ever. Merry Christmas!"

A Merry Christmas for Mice

It was Christmas Eve, and Cinderella was feeling very lonely. Her stepmother and stepsisters had gone to spend the holiday with their cousins. As Cinderella sat by herself in the empty house, she remembered how she and her father had loved decorating their home and wrapping gifts. She thought of the friends who would come to visit for the holiday and the love that had always filled their happy home. A tear rolled down Cinderella's cheek.

"Cinderelly sad?" Jaq asked.

Cinderella nodded. "It's Christmas Eve," she said, "though you would never know it. Look. There's not a decoration in sight!"

"Not too late," said Gus. "Let's get to work, Cinderelly!"

Cinderella smiled. "You're right," she said. "Why should the fact that we've been left home alone get us down?"

The mice cheered. Then, calling their bird friends, they set off to gather pine cones, holly, and mistletoe from the forest.

Cinderella found and cut down a small tree, which her dog, Bruno, hauled home on a sled. She and her friends hung apples and colorful strands of berries on the branches.

"We gonna eat good Christmas dinner?" asked Gus when the tree was done.

"Oh, dear," Cinderella said with a sigh. "You all must be very hungry."

Cinderella set to work at once making an apple pie. The mice happily crowded around her as she worked.

With a roaring fire in the fireplace and a delicious dessert baking in the oven, Cinderella realized that it did seem like Christmas after all.

"Thank you for sharing my Christmas," she told the mice and birds. "I was so sad this morning, but now I am happy to have had such a wonderful holiday with you."

"We had good holiday, too, Cinderelly," Jaq said. The other mice nodded in agreement. "Waitee, waitee, Cinderelly!" said Jaq with a wide grin.

"Gotta open giftee," said Gus. He pulled out a small package from behind his back.

Cinderella opened it. "How beautiful!" she exclaimed. Using old ribbons, the mice had woven a tiara, which sparkled with tiny beads.

When Cinderella put it on, the mice cried, "A princess! A princess! She's a princess!"

"You're *our* princess, Cinderelly," said Jaq.

Cinderella looked down at her adoring friends and smiled happily. It was a merry Christmas after all.

17

Dumbo's Christmas Flight

Dumbo stared out the window of his train car. It was almost Christmas, but he didn't feel very merry. In fact, he was worried. The circus train would be traveling on Christmas Eve. What if Santa Claus couldn't find them?

"Aw, come on, little guy," said Timothy Q. Mouse. "I know you're worried, but Santy Claus always finds us, honest! He fills my stocking with peanuts every single year. He's never missed a one, no matter where we are!"

But Dumbo still just stared out the window. Timothy was determined to help his friend feel better. He thought and thought. Suddenly, he snapped his fingers.

"Say, I've got it! Why don't we fly to the North Pole and see Santy Claus ourselves?"

Dumbo smiled and nodded happily. Timothy jumped into the little elephant's hat, and the two took off.

After soaring north for a long time, the two spotted Santa's workshop. Elves and reindeer stood huddled together, looking up at the building. Dumbo could tell something was wrong.

"Hey, everybody. What're we looking at?" Timothy asked when they landed.

"It's the toy chute!" an elf explained, pointing at the top of the building. "The toys we make get to Santa's sleigh by traveling through a door at the top of the workshop and down the chute, but something is stuck inside the tunnel! None of us can get it unstuck, and the rest of the toys can't get through!"

"Can't someone just pull it loose?" Timothy asked.

The elf shook his head. "The reindeer tried, but the door is too little—their antlers keep getting stuck. And it's Christmas Eve! Santa's supposed to be leaving soon."

Dumbo realized that if Santa had to leave without those toys, some children wouldn't be getting Christmas presents. He had to help!

With a flap of his ears he flew up to the little door. He couldn't fit his whole body through—but he had a long trunk that seemed just right for the job! Dumbo reached in and felt a little doll whose hair ribbons had gotten tangled. His trunk worked quickly to unknot them, and the toys began to move down the chute again.

Everyone cheered when Dumbo landed back on the ground. Then he heard a voice from behind him.

"Ho, ho, ho! Thank you for fixing our toy chute, Dumbo!"

"You know who Dumbo is?" Timothy asked Santa Claus.

"Of course, Timothy," Santa replied. "I have to know who everyone is so I can pick out the right Christmas presents. It's Christmas magic." He turned to the little elephant. "And that includes knowing where you are on Christmas Eve, Dumbo, even if you're traveling."

Santa looked at his sleigh. "Thanks to you, Dumbo, it looks like we're ready to go. Say, would you like to fly with us?"

"Golly, would we!" squeaked Timothy. Dumbo nodded enthusiastically.

"Then off we go! First stop, the circus train!" called Santa.

And so it was that the eight tiny reindeer, one elephant, and one mouse took off into the sky to deliver presents to all the little girls and boys. And they didn't miss a one!

18

Snow Puppies

The Dalmatian puppies were confused. A few days earlier, Roger had brought a tree into the house and hung sparkly balls on it. Now Nanny was putting some boxes with bows beneath the tree. "What is she doing?" Patch asked his parents, Pongo and Perdita.

"Why, it's Christmas," Perdita said.

"Humans give presents at Christmas to show that they care about each other," Pongo explained.

"Let's give our humans a present," Lucky said.

"I know just what to give them!" Rolly shouted, excited. He ran off and fetched his best bone. "Roger and Anita will love it!"

Lucky laughed. "Humans don't chew bones, silly," he said.

Later, on their afternoon walk, the puppies saw a group of children playing in the snow. As Lucky watched the children, he smiled. He knew just what to get their humans.

When they returned home, Lucky started digging in the snow. "Watch me, and do what I do," he told his siblings.

The other puppies watched as Lucky made a giant snowball. Slowly, he began to dig out a puppy shape in the snow.

The puppies grinned. Lucky was right. This *was* the perfect gift.

All afternoon, the little Dalmatians dug and rolled and scooped and scraped snow into little snow puppy shapes. Freckles, Patch, and Penny found sticks for tails. Rolly found coal for the snow puppies' eyes and noses. But the snow puppies still didn't seem right.

"There's something missing," Lucky said.

Suddenly, Lucky noticed a trail of black paw prints leading from the coal shed across the snowy yard. "That's it! Our snow puppies need spots!" he shouted.

"Rub your paws in the coal dust," Lucky told the others. "Then you can put black spots on the snow puppies."

The puppies ran into the coal shed. Then they bounded over to their snow puppies. Working busily, the Dalmatians covered their creations with tons of black spots.

Soon it was time for the puppies to go back inside.

After dinner, Nanny read the puppies a Christmas story and tucked them into bed. The puppies were so excited that they wiggled and giggled for a long time. Finally, they fell fast asleep.

On Christmas morning, Roger, Anita, and Nanny gave the puppies their gifts. Each one got a rubber ball, a bone, and a nice, new red sweater.

The puppies loved the presents, but they couldn't wait any longer to give their own.

Lucky ran to the door and began to bark.

"I think he wants us to follow them," Roger said.

When they stepped outside, Roger and Anita began to cheer. In their front yard sat 101 beautiful Dalmatian snow puppies.

Nanny laughed so hard she sat down right in the snow. "Why, that's one hundred and one of the best Christmas gifts I've ever gotten," she said, hugging as many puppies as she could hold.

And everyone agreed that it was so.

December 19

Christmas in Monstropolis

Mike was excited. He was in charge of decorating Monstropolis for Christmas.

Mike pictured the city glowing from top to bottom. And to top it off, he planned to set up a huge Christmas tree in the center of the city.

Sulley nervously looked over Mike's plans. "This is going to take a lot of laugh power," he said. "Maybe we can skip some of these lights."

"*Skip* lights?" Mike asked. "We need *more* lights!"

On Christmas Eve, Monstropolis shone brightly. In the city center, hundreds of monsters gathered to witness the tree lighting. There was even a TV crew waiting to film the event!

"See, Sulley?" Mike said. "The power is just fine. And you were worried. . . ."

Suddenly, the Christmas lights went out. Mike looked around. The power had gone out across the whole city!

"What's going on, Wazowski?" the monsters yelled.

"We'll have this fixed in a jiffy!" Mike shouted.

Sulley wasn't so sure. "The factory is closed, and everyone's on vacation," he whispered. "How are we going to generate enough power?"

"We're going to need to get some substitute Laugh Collectors," Mike said. He scanned the crowd for familiar faces. "Smitty, Needleman," he called. "Over here! Come on. We need your help."

"We'll probably need five cans to power up the city and light the tree," Sulley said when they got to the factory. He looked at the clock. "And we've got about an hour to pull it off."

Smitty and Needleman were nervous. They didn't know any jokes.

"Don't worry. I've got a million of 'em," Mike said. He quickly scribbled down some jokes and handed them to the monsters.

Mike ran through door after door, collecting laughs. But Smitty and Needleman were getting nowhere. They couldn't even get one little chuckle!

"You stink!" Smitty said.

"*I* stink?" Needleman said loudly, waking the girl whose room they had entered.

Needleman gave Smitty a little push. Smitty tried to push Needleman back, but Needleman stepped out of the way. Smitty tumbled to the floor with a thud.

The girl howled with laughter.

"Whatever you did in there worked!" Sulley said when the two stepped back onto the Laugh Floor. "You just filled a whole can! Let's hope it's enough. We're out of time. The ceremony is about to start, with or without us!"

The monsters raced back to the city center. The lights had come back on, but had they collected enough laughs to light the tree, too? Mike took a deep breath and flipped the switch. Nothing happened.

"Uh, Mike?" Smitty said. He held up the power cord. The tree wasn't plugged in!

Mike quickly plugged in the cord. The lights flicked on. Everyone gasped in wonder. The tree was magnificent!

"You did it, Mike!" Sulley said.

Mike shook his head. "You mean *we* did it. Merry Christmas, Monstropolis!"

Wreck the Halls

"**T**a-da! A sugar angel!" Vanellope von Schweetz exclaimed proudly.

Ralph smiled weakly. Vanellope could tell something was bothering him. "Hey, Ralph, what's wrong?" she asked.

Ralph explained that, for the first time ever, the Nicelanders had invited him to their holiday party. "The party was great," Ralph told Vanellope. "But I kept thinking about how lonely the other Bad Guys must be."

"You're right," Vanellope said. "Let's throw the Bad Guys a Christmas party!"

Ralph's face lit up. He called a special meeting of the Bad-Anon support group and told the Bad Guys how wonderful Christmas could be. "Meet back here on Christmas Eve," Ralph instructed them.

Ralph and Vanellope wasted no time. They immediately began making gifts and decorating the perfect lollipop tree for their friends.

"How are we going to carry all this?" Ralph asked, pointing at the pile of presents.

"The same way Santa does it," Vanellope cried. "In a sleigh, of course!"

The friends headed to the kart bakery to create the perfect Christmas kart.

"One rocket-powered candy sleigh, ready to go," Vanellope declared as their vehicle slid out of the finisher. "Let's get this thing moving!"

Ralph couldn't wait to get to the party. As they took off, he reached for the rocket switches. But his hand was too big. He snapped the switches in half! Only one rocket turned on—and the sleigh spun out of control!

Vanellope tried to regain control of the runaway sleigh, but it was no use! The rocket spiraled down until—*gloop!*—it landed in Great Caramel Lake. The sleigh and all the presents were ruined.

Empty-handed and covered in caramel, Ralph and Vanellope had to deliver the bad news to the Bad Guys.

"I've wrecked their Christmas," Ralph said.

Vanellope knew the crash had been an accident, but still, their plans *were* ruined. "Time to face the music, big guy," she said, shaking her head.

When Ralph and Vanellope opened the door to the support group room, the friends' jaws dropped. The room was completely decked out!

The Bad Guys greeted them with a big cheer. "How did you do all this?" Ralph asked in amazement.

"We spent the last few days getting everything ready!" Sorceress said.

"Vanellope and I made presents and trimmed a tree, but I crashed the sled," Ralph said sadly. "I wrecked everything."

"Don't be silly. You got us all in the Christmas spirit," Satine said. "You're the reason we're here—spending the holiday together. That's the best present of all!"

The other Bad Guys nodded in agreement.

A wide smile spread across Ralph's face. "Merry Christmas, everyone!"

And as they all celebrated late into the night, Ralph had to admit, it truly was the merriest Christmas any of them had ever had.

A Meow-y Christmas

"Look, Father—it's snowing!" Pinocchio exclaimed.

"I guess that means it's time to get ready for Christmas," Geppetto said.

Figaro meowed. He couldn't wait for Christmas!

Geppetto and Pinocchio got right to work decorating the workshop. When they hung stockings on the mantel, Figaro jumped at their feet. He wanted to help, too, but he couldn't reach.

"Great job, Pinocchio!" Geppetto said. Stepping back, he nearly tripped over the kitten. "Figaro, be careful," Geppetto cautioned.

Next father and son decorated the Christmas tree. "All that's left is for you put the star on the top, Pinocchio," Geppetto told his son.

Figaro frowned. *He* wanted to put the star on top of the Christmas tree.

Later Geppetto started making Christmas Eve supper.

"Ohhhh, it smells good in here," Pinocchio said.

"Yes! And now it's time for the—Figaro!" Geppetto scolded the kitty, who was about to take a bite of the Christmas goose. "It is not time to eat yet!"

Feeling hurt and left out, Figaro crept to the bedroom. He would spend Christmas where no one could find him: beneath Geppetto's bed.

Under the bed, he noticed a large pile of presents. Not one was for him!

Just then, the kitten heard Geppetto call, "Figaro, Cleo—we'll be back soon!"

First Geppetto hadn't gotten him any presents, and now Geppetto and Pinocchio were off to have a Christmas adventure without him? That was the last straw. If Figaro couldn't enjoy Christmas, he didn't want anyone else to, either!

When the door closed, Figaro clawed the wrapping paper on the presents to pieces. Then he leaped at the Christmas tree, knocking all the ornaments to the ground.

Just as Figaro was about to sink his teeth into the Christmas goose, he heard Jiminy Cricket.

"Figaro," Jiminy shouted. "The Blue Fairy is none too pleased by your behavior. And who knows what Santa thinks? How will Geppetto and Pinocchio feel when they see the mess you've made?"

Figaro was ashamed. He knew Jiminy was right.

"It's not too late to make things right," Jiminy continued. "I'll help you."

Figaro licked Jiminy's face gratefully, and the two got to work repairing the damage the little kitty had done. They rewrapped the presents, spruced up the tree, and redecorated the room.

Figaro even added his own holiday decorations. Soon the place sparkled and twinkled brightly.

When Geppetto and Pinocchio came home, they were amazed.

"Figaro, this place looks wonderful!" Pinocchio cried.

Geppetto agreed. "I'd say you've earned your Christmas present early." And with that, he showed Figaro what he and Pinocchio had gone out to get. "Fresh cream!"

Figaro was overjoyed. Pinocchio and Geppetto hadn't forgotten him after all!

Later that evening, as they all gathered around the table for their Christmas Eve supper, Figaro sighed happily. He realized that Christmas wasn't about gifts or being the one to hang the decorations. It was about spending time with family. And there was nowhere else he'd rather be.

22

The Holiday Gift Hunt

Ariel and Eric were enjoying a nice walk along the beach when their dog, Max, ran up to them. He was carrying a waterlogged boot.

"Max!" Eric cried. "I've been searching for that boot for months!"

"Burying things and digging them up *is* his favorite game," Ariel said. The princess smiled. At least now she knew what to give Eric for Christmas!

When Ariel and Eric returned to the castle, Carlotta told them it was time for tea.

"Already?" asked Grimsby, checking his pocket watch. "Hmm . . . must be broken."

Ariel smiled. Now she knew what to get Grimbsy, too!

"Isn't the Christmas tree beautiful?" Ariel remarked. "Carlotta suggested we use red and gold ornaments this year."

"Those *are* my favorite colors, you know," Carlotta replied.

The next day, Ariel went into town to look for Christmas gifts. She bought a new pair of boots and a ship in a bottle for Eric, an elegant pocket watch for Grimsby, and a gold and ruby necklace for Carlotta. Max's present was easy. She bought him the biggest bone she could find!

Back at the castle, Ariel was wrapping the gifts when she noticed that Max's bone was missing. Suddenly, she heard a loud chewing noise coming from behind a chair. Max was gnawing happily on the bone she had gotten for him.

"No opening presents early, Max!" Ariel scolded. Then, picking up her wrapped presents, she hid them under the bed.

On Christmas morning, Ariel went to get her gifts, but

there was nothing under the bed! The gifts were missing.

"Ariel!" Eric called. "It's time for presents!"

Ariel joined Eric by the tree. "Is it all right if we exchange gifts later?" she asked. "I told my friends I'd meet them on the beach."

"Of course," Eric replied. "Come on, everyone. We're going down to the water for a Christmas visit."

Flounder, Sebastian, and Scuttle were waiting for Ariel on the beach.

Scuttle handed Ariel a small chest. "We thought these *whatchamajinglys* would come in handy now that you live on land."

Ariel opened the lid and saw the sort of treasures she had loved to collect when she was a mermaid. "Thank you!" she said. "I love them! They're just wonderful!"

Just then, Max ran up holding a boot. "Your present!" Ariel said to Eric. Now she knew where the missing gifts were. Max had buried them!

"Surprise, everyone!" Ariel said. "We're going on a treasure hunt!"

"Ariel, you are amazing!" Eric said. "Only you could turn the holidays into a brand-new adventure."

Soon Eric, Carlotta, Max, and Grimsby were digging around on the beach. Each time a present was found, Scuttle delivered it to its owner. The treasure hunt was the most fun anyone could remember having on Christmas morning in a very long time.

"We should have a Christmas treasure hunt every year!" Eric told Ariel when all the gifts were found.

Ariel smiled. It had been a day full of surprises, but she had learned that sometimes the most unexpected treasures were the best.

December 23

Christmas Traditions

Lady was excited. This was her first Christmas with the puppies—and with Tramp.

"I can't wait to teach the puppies all about Christmas," she told Tramp.

"Teach?" Tramp asked. "Doesn't Christmas just show up one morning?"

"Well, yes," Lady admitted. "But Christmas is about more than just one day of the year. It's about all the things we do together—as a family. Just wait until you see the tree all lit up," she told him. "It's magical. Jim Dear brings home a giant tree for us to decorate, and then we hang our stockings by the fire. . . ."

Tramp looked confused. "Why would you hang up stockings?" he asked.

"For Santa Claus to fill with presents," Lady replied. "Then there's caroling and ice-skating and building snowmen. Of course, my favorite part is Christmas dinner. We all sit together and have the most wonderful meal."

"It sounds like quite the celebration, Pidge," Tramp said.

"Oh, it is!" Lady said. "What's your favorite tradition?"

"I never really celebrated Christmas," Tramp told her. "On the streets, it was just another day and just another meal. Although the scraps *were* much better than usual."

"Well, all that has changed now," Lady said. "I just know you'll love our holiday traditions, and the puppies will, too."

Just then, Lady and Tramp's puppies ran up. "Mama, Mama," Scamp shouted. "Why is Jim Dear bringing a tree *inside*?"

"Christmas, my darlings," Lady answered with a smile.

On Christmas morning, the pups awoke to find their stockings stuffed. Santa Claus had come, and he had brought them wonderful gifts!

Later that evening, Jim Dear greeted Aunt Sarah. "We're so glad you could come for dinner."

Aunt Sarah smiled and set down her Siamese cats, who slowly slipped into the dining room.

"We should keep an eye on them," Lady told Tramp. "You never know—"

CRASH!

"Oh, no!" Lady cried, rushing into the dining room. The cats had knocked over the dishes and scattered food everywhere!

"Christmas dinner is ruined," Lady said sadly.

But Darling had seen everything. She knew the cats were the cause of the trouble.

Aunt Sarah apologized, locked the cats in their carrier, and helped clean up the mess.

"I'm sorry about dinner, Pidge," Tramp said.

"It's my favorite holiday tradition, and now I don't get to share it with you and the little ones," Lady said sadly.

Suddenly, Tramp had an idea. "Come on," he said. "Let's gather the family. I just realized: I *do* have a Christmas tradition to share with you after all."

A short while later, the family walked into Tony's Restaurant.

"Eh, Butch'a!" Tony cried when he saw them walk in. "Welcome to Christmas dinner! We were wondering if we would see you this year. And look! With such a beautiful family!"

"This is perfect," Lady told Tramp as they all sat down to a delicious Italian Christmas dinner.

"Merry Christmas," Tramp said. "May all of our traditions continue for many years!"

A Big Blue Christmas

"**D**ad, wake up!" Nemo shouted early one morning as he swam around their anemone.

"What is it, Nemo?" Marlin asked, waking in a hurry. "Are you hurt?"

"No, Dad," the little clownfish answered. "I have an idea! It's almost Christmas. Could we have a holiday party?

"Sounds like fun, Nemo," Marlin said with a yawn. "But maybe we can wait until after breakfast to start planning?"

Nemo and Marlin made a long list of friends to invite. "I'll ask Bruce, Chum, and Anchor to help spread the word," Nemo said. "No one can say no to those guys!"

Nemo swam as fast as he could to find his shark friends.

"What brings you out this way, Nemo?" Chum asked his buddy. The little clownfish told them all about the Christmas party he wanted to throw and what he needed from them. "Can you help me tell everyone about it?" he asked.

"You can count on us," Bruce said proudly.

"Thanks," said Nemo. "And, guys, remember . . ."

"Fish are friends, not food," they all said together.

"We know. Don't worry," Bruce said.

Sure the guest list was in good hands, Nemo set out to find some music for the party. He soon came across his pals from school.

Pearl, Tad, and Sheldon had a band. They agreed to play at the party.

Next Nemo went to visit his old pals from the Tank Gang. Deb, the black-and-white humbug fish, got to work on the food. Jacques, the cleaner shrimp, followed Nemo home. He cleaned the anemone until it sparkled.

Finally, Nemo found his favorite forgetful friend, Dory.

"Nemo! I've missed you!" said Dory.

"Would you like to help us decorate for a party?" Nemo said.

"Oooh, I love parties," Dory said. "At least, I think I love parties. Do I? I must. Who doesn't love a party? Though I can't remember if I've ever been to one. . . ."

That afternoon, Dory, Marlin, and Nemo hung streamers and wreaths and decorated a conch-shell Christmas tree. Finally, it was time for the party!

"Merry Christmas," Nemo told Dory.

"Thanks," said Dory. "I just ran into some sharks and they told me there was going to be a party here tonight. Hey, these decorations look amazing. Who did them?"

"You did, Dory," Nemo said.

Dory looked around appreciatively. "Wow, I'm good," she said.

Nemo laughed and then went to greet the rest of his guests. Seeing all of his friends together filled Nemo with holiday cheer. Everyone started singing and dancing as the band played "We Wish You a Merry Fishmas." It was the perfect party.

When the last of the guests had gone, Nemo turned to his father and smiled. "Dad, this was the best Christmas ever."

"You bet it was," said Marlin. "We sure are lucky to have so many good friends. But the best gift of all is spending Christmas with you."

Nemo agreed. "Merry Christmas, Dad!" And he gave his father a big hug.

December 25

Santa's Little Helper

It was Christmas Eve, and all was quiet. Mickey was almost asleep when he heard a sound in the yard. Mickey ran to the window. Santa Claus was standing outside. And he was sneezing!

"Santa! What's wrong?" Mickey asked.

"It's this cold! I need to get home to bed, but we still have four houses to visit," Santa said.

"Gee," Mickey said. "Maybe Pluto and I can help. We'd be happy to deliver the presents for you!"

"Oh, thank you, Mickey! The magic from my bag will help you!" Santa said. Then, setting down his bag, Santa climbed back into his sleigh and went home.

Mickey pulled his sled from the garage and hauled it over to the giant bag of gifts. The sled rose into the air. In no time, it landed on Daisy's roof.

Holding the Christmas bag over his shoulder, Mickey walked to the chimney. "Santa goes down the chimney. Should I try?" he said.

Before Pluto could answer, Mickey was sliding down the chimney into Daisy's living room!

Mickey quickly arranged the gifts under the tree. He was just leaving when he saw the treats Daisy had left for Santa. "I'm sure she wouldn't mind if I ate them," Mickey said.

When he got back to the roof, Mickey realized he had forgotten to get a cookie for Pluto. "I'm sorry, Pluto! I'll get you a treat at the next house," he said.

Next Mickey went to Goofy's house. As Mickey leaned into Goofy's chimney, Pluto grabbed the back of the bag in his teeth and went down the chimney, too. He didn't want to miss getting a treat this time!

"Pluto!" Mickey said. "I promised that I'd bring you a—oh, no! Look out!"

As Pluto ran toward the cookies, he accidentally knocked down Goofy's tree! Mickey fixed it as best he could, but the tree was still crooked. "Maybe he won't notice," Mickey said.

Mickey very carefully filled Goofy's stocking and placed his presents under the tree. Then he and Pluto went back up the chimney.

At Minnie's house, Mickey quickly pulled her gifts from Santa's bag and placed them under her tree. Fixing Goofy's tree had taken a while, and he was running out of time.

Mickey's last stop was Donald's house. "Uh-oh," he said when he reached into Santa's bag. "There are supposed to be four gifts, but there are only three left in the bag! Did I drop one somewhere?"

As he was looking around, Mickey heard Donald's footsteps upstairs. Mickey grabbed Santa's bag and raced up the chimney. Donald would just have to live without his last gift.

The next morning, Mickey's friends gathered at his house. It seemed like everyone had a story about Santa's visit!

"Santa wasn't quite himself last night," Daisy said. "He left soot all over my floor!"

"I think Santa bumped into my tree. It looked a little lopsided this morning," Goofy told Minnie.

"He left one of Donald's presents at my house," Minnie said.

"He woke me up with all the noise he was making downstairs!" Donald exclaimed.

Suddenly, Mickey realized he had left Santa's bag by his Christmas tree. But when he went to hide it, all he found was a box with a tag that said LOVE, SANTA. Inside was a snow globe of Pluto and Mickey riding with Santa in his sleigh.

Mickey winked at Pluto. "No, Santa Claus definitely wasn't himself last night!" he said. "Merry Christmas, everyone!"

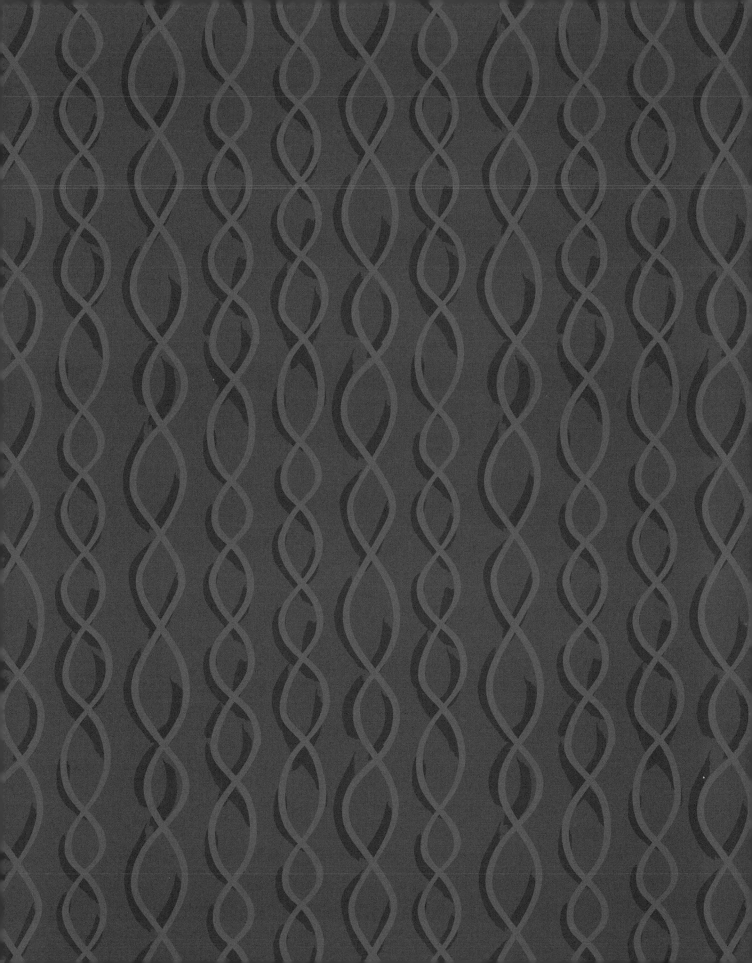

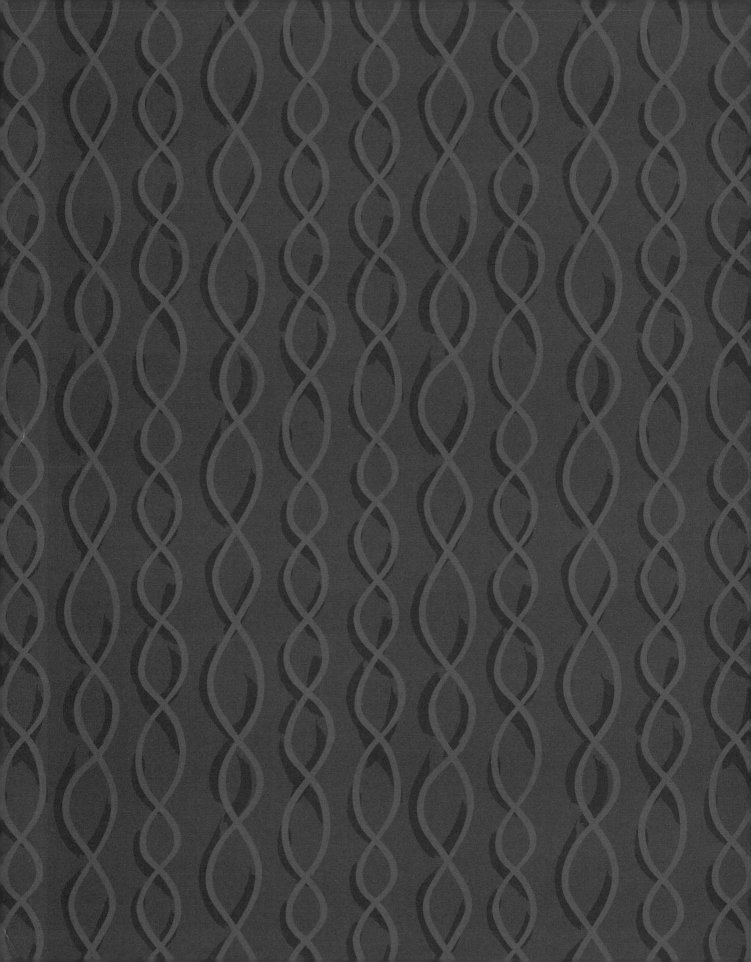

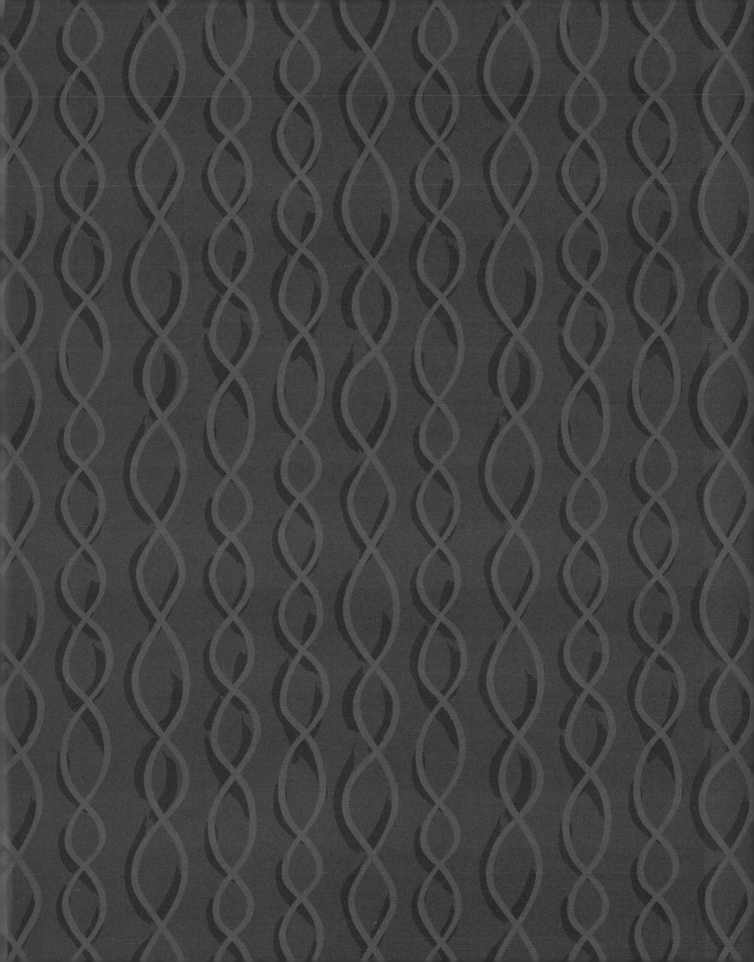

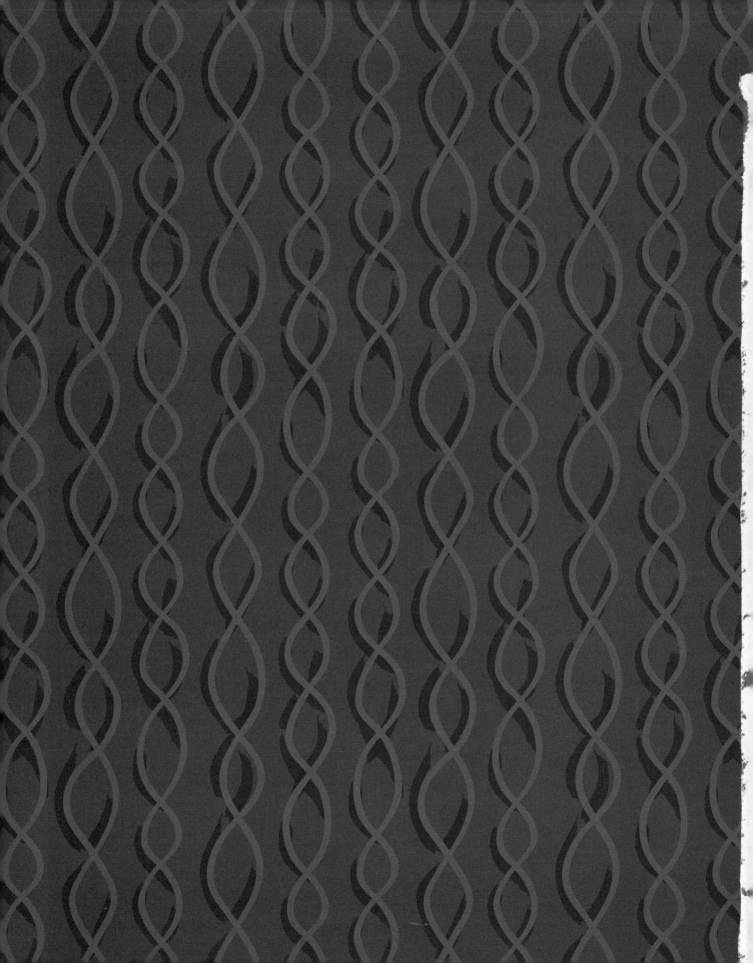